Disney · PIXAR
THE INCREDIBLES

Illustrated by the Disney Storybook Artists

Published by
Louis Weber, C.E.O.
Publications International, Ltd.
7373 North Cicero Avenue, Lincolnwood, Illinois 60712

Ground Floor, 59 Gloucester Place, London W1U 8JJ

Customer Service: 1-800-595-8484 or customer_service@pilbooks.com

www.pilbooks.com

p i kids is a registered trademark of Publications International, Ltd.
ISBN-13: 978-1-4127-9456-5
ISBN-10: 1-4127-9456-0

During the golden age of Supers, there were heroes everywhere. The Supers stopped bad guys and rescued people who were in trouble. No matter how large or small the problem, the Supers were up to the task. Two of the greatest Supers were Mr. Incredible and Elastigirl.

All Supers had a secret identity that they kept secret from the rest of the world. Their identities were important to the Supers. Without them, criminals could attack when it was least expected.

One day, Mr. Incredible was battling a bad guy when a boy interrupted him.

"I'm Incrediboy!" the boy, Buddy, said. "I'm your number-one fan. I have these rocket boots."

"Go home," said Mr. Incredible. "I work alone."

"You always say to be true to yourself," said Buddy.

"You have officially carried it too far, Buddy," Mr. Incredible said.

But Buddy wouldn't listen. He tried to show Mr. Incredible that he didn't need Super powers to be a hero. Instead, Buddy flew out of control on his rocket boots. Mr. Incredible had to save Buddy, and ended up doing a lot of damage to the city in the process.

People started to get upset at the amount of damage the Supers' battles caused. The city decided it didn't want Supers to help anymore. The Supers were asked to stop fighting crime. They had to live normal lives like everybody else.

Later, Mr. Incredible and Elastigirl were married. Since they had to lead normal lives, they used the normal names of Bob and Helen Parr.

Years passed and the Parrs had three children: Violet, who could become invisible and create force fields; Dash, who could run faster than a speeding bullet; and Jack-Jack, who didn't seem to have any Super powers at all. They argued like any normal family, but they weren't normal. They were Supers.

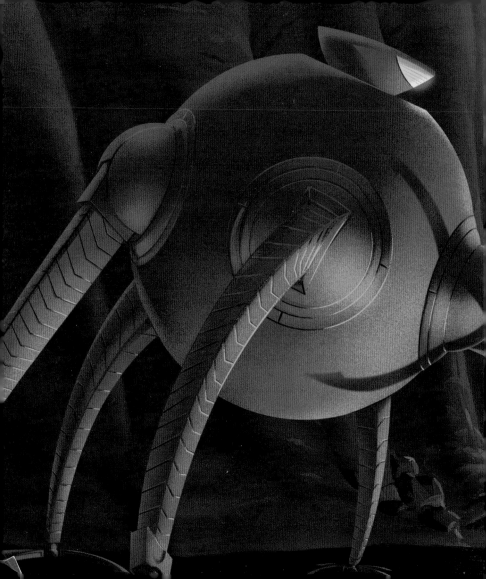

Bob was frustrated at trying to live the life of a normal man. At night, when he was supposed to go bowling, he would fight crime and rescue people in secret.

One day Bob was contacted by a mysterious woman named Mirage. She told him that he could still be a Super. She invited him to come get rid of a problem for her and her boss.

Bob was flown to the secret island of Nomanisan. There he battled a robot, the Omnidroid 9000. The Omnidroid was a special kind of robot that was able to learn its enemies' weaknesses in order to defeat them.

Bob was out of shape, but he was still stronger and smarter than the Omnidroid. After a difficult fight, Bob was eventually able to defeat the Omnidroid. Bob knew he needed to get in shape.

Mirage contacted Bob again soon after he defeated the Omnidroid 9000. Dressed in a new-and-improved suit that his friend Edna made for him, he arrived to battle a new Omnidroid. The robot grabbed Bob and was squeezing him tight. It appeared Mr. Incredible had met his match.

Then a familiar face appeared. It was Buddy! Except now he was a villain known as Syndrome!

Syndrome explained his plan to get rid of the real Supers so he would be the only hero left to save the world when it was in peril.

Helen discovered that Bob was fighting crime again and decided to go confront him about it. However, Helen soon realized that Bob was in trouble and rushed to help.

Once on the island, Helen and the kids rescued Bob. He told them about Syndrome's plan to use the Omnidroid on the city. Syndrome planned to stop the robot himself so that he would look like the hero.

Once back in the
city, the Incredibles discovered that
Syndrome had lost control of the Omnidroid.
It was completely destroying the city. With the
help of their old Super friend, Frozone, the
Incredibles teamed up to destroy the robot.
Syndrome tried to escape, but the Incredibles
made sure that he couldn't cause any more trouble.